Odd (

MW01122604

Contents

written by Rosalind Hayhoe
photographs by Claire Watkins

1

Look at these toy cars.
We can make a set of cars
that are all the same color.

Which one is different?
The green car is not the
same color as the others.
It is the odd one out.

Look at the shape of the
fruit in this round bowl.
We can put all the round
fruit together in a set.

The bananas are a different shape from the other fruit. They are the odd ones out.

Here are five pairs of shoes.
We can make a set of shoes
that are the same size.

The two little baby shoes
are the odd ones out.
They are a different size
from all the other shoes.

Can you see which balls
have the same pattern?
Which one is the odd
one out?

We can put the three spotted balls in a set. The striped ball has a different pattern.

Which pencils are the same?
Can you see which one is
the odd one out?

The long pencils make a set.
The short pencil is different
from the long ones.

Look at these different toys.
Which ones can we put
together in a set?

Toys with wheels make a set. The toys without wheels are the odd ones out.

Look at all these hats.
Which one is a different
kind of hat?

The cap is not the same
kind as the other hats.
It is the odd one out.

Can you make a set from some of these boxes? Which one will be the odd one out?